ANIMAL BOOK

For Miles and Eddie, with uncompromising love—J. S.-W.
For Sylvie and for Lucy, for letting me get away with it—B. B.

SIMON & SCHUSTER BOOKS FOR YOUNG READERS
An imprint of Simon & Schuster Children's Publishing Division
1230 Avenue of the Americas, New York, New York 10020

Book design by Brian Biggs & Lucy Ruth Cummins
The text for this book was set in Century Schoolbook.
The illustrations in this book were rendered in ink, crayon,
and digital color, and not a small amount of impertinence.
Manufactured in China
0717 SCP
First Edition
2 4 6 8 10 9 7 5 3 1
CIP data for this book is available from the Library of Congress.
ISBN 978-1-4814-3922-0
ISBN 978-1-4814-3923-7 (eBook)

This is NOT a normal ANIMAL BOOK

BY JULIE SEGAL-WALTERS
PICTURES BY BRIAN BIGGS

(aren't they pretty?)

A Paula Wiseman Book
SIMON & SCHUSTER BOOKS FOR YOUNG READERS
New York London Toronto Sydney New Delhi

Animals can be classified into groups by their unique traits.

Here are some examples of each category:

This is a cat.

If the cat laid an egg . . .

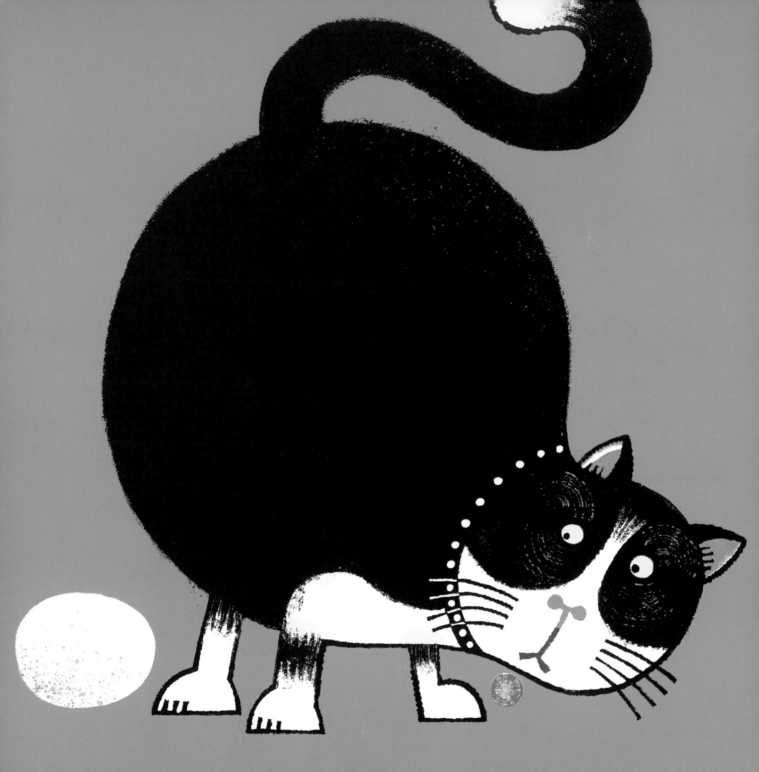

it would be a hen.

A HEN!

oh, sorry!

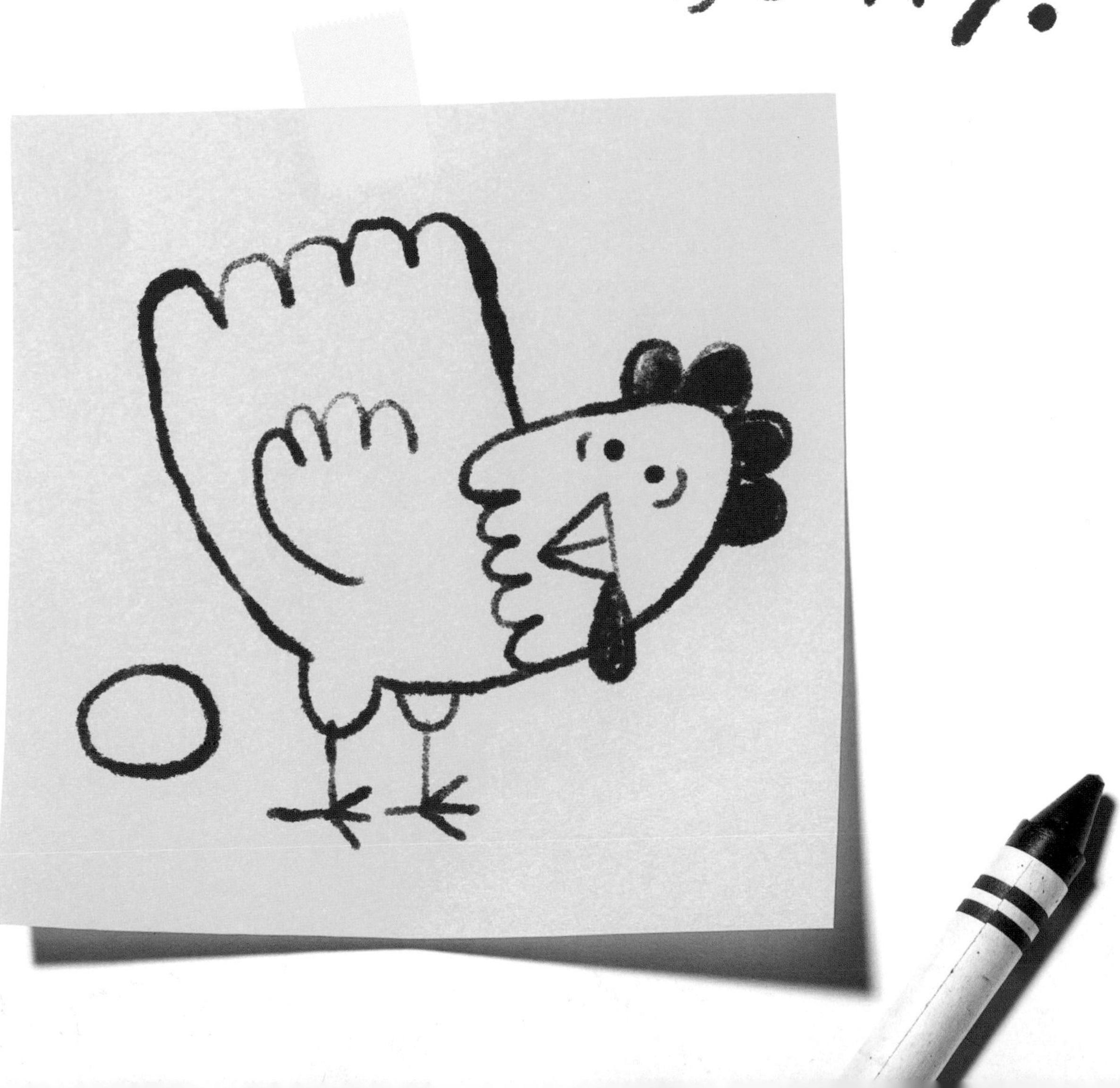

If the hen hopped on lily pads . . .

it would be a frog.

Yes . . . it would be a FROG!

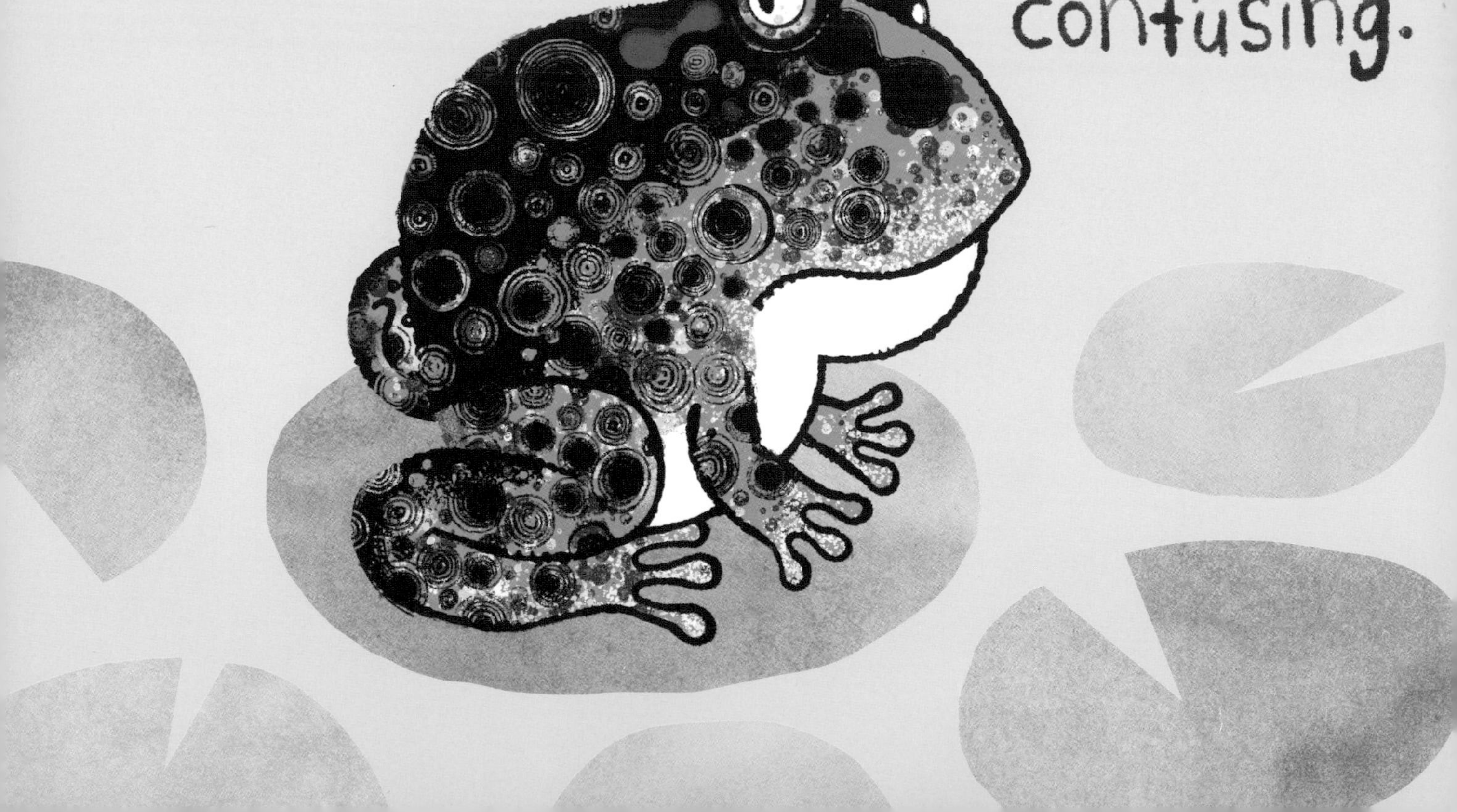
This is SO confusing.

If the frog made honey . . .

HONEY?

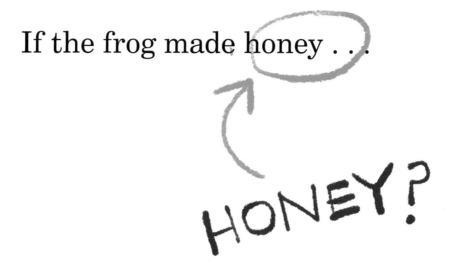

it would be a bee.

Just a BEE!

An insect-that-
collects-nectar-from-flowers
BEE—*buzz, buzz!*

Take it easy.
I'm doing the
best I can.

If the bee slithered and hissed . . .

Oh, come on.

it would be a snake.
A plain green garter snake!
With a stripe down its back!

Look. You Write the
Words YOUR way.
I'll draw the pictures
MY way.

If the FRUSTRATED-BY-LACK-OF-COOPERATION snake swam deep in the ocean . . .

it would be a blobfish.

Wait a second.
Did you say,
"BLOBFISH"?

I don't want to draw a BLOBFISH.

I take back what I said about your way and my way.

Can We Work this out?

You need all
kinds of animals,
right?

- ✓ Mammal
- ✓ Bird
- ✓ Amphibian
- ✓ Insect
- ✓ Reptile

Check. Now you need a FISH.
Got it.

A SHARK is a fish!
Couldn't you just say,
"It would be a Shark"?

It's FUN to draw sharks.

It would be a
BLOB—because I said so—FISH!

What about a **SUNFISH**?

Doesn't SUNFISH sound better than BLOBfish?

SUN

So happy and bright.

BLOB

so BLOBBY

I may as well plop some JELLY on the page.
There.
There's your BLOBFISH.

IT. WOULD. BE. A. BLOBFISH!

Okay... FINE...

Let's move on.

If the WHY-CAN'T-THE-ART-PLEASE-LOOK-LIKE-THE-ANIMAL blobfish stood . . .

Don't get upset!

I just don't want to
DRAW a blobfish.

WAIT! I have an idea.
Try your line again.

It would be a blobfish. →

Better?

If the very-relieved-and-grateful blobfish stood . . .

OH BOY.
Now I can't
think of anything
besides that
BLOBFISH.

Try getting
THAT
image out of
your head.

You can't, can you?

That blobfish will
stick in your mind
for a long, long time.

You'll be going about your business, then

POW!

BLOBFISH!

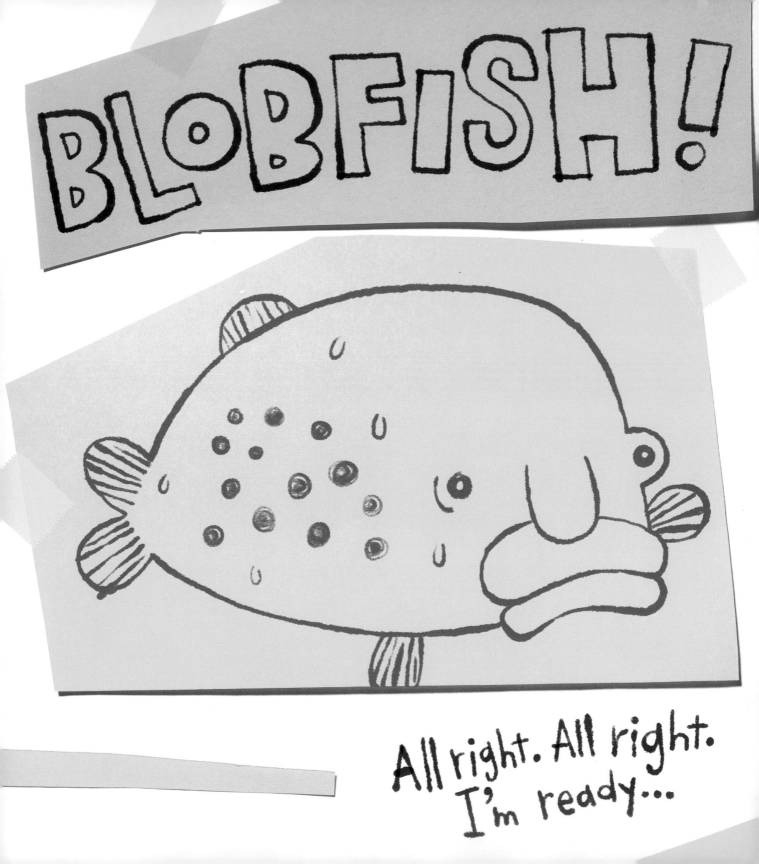

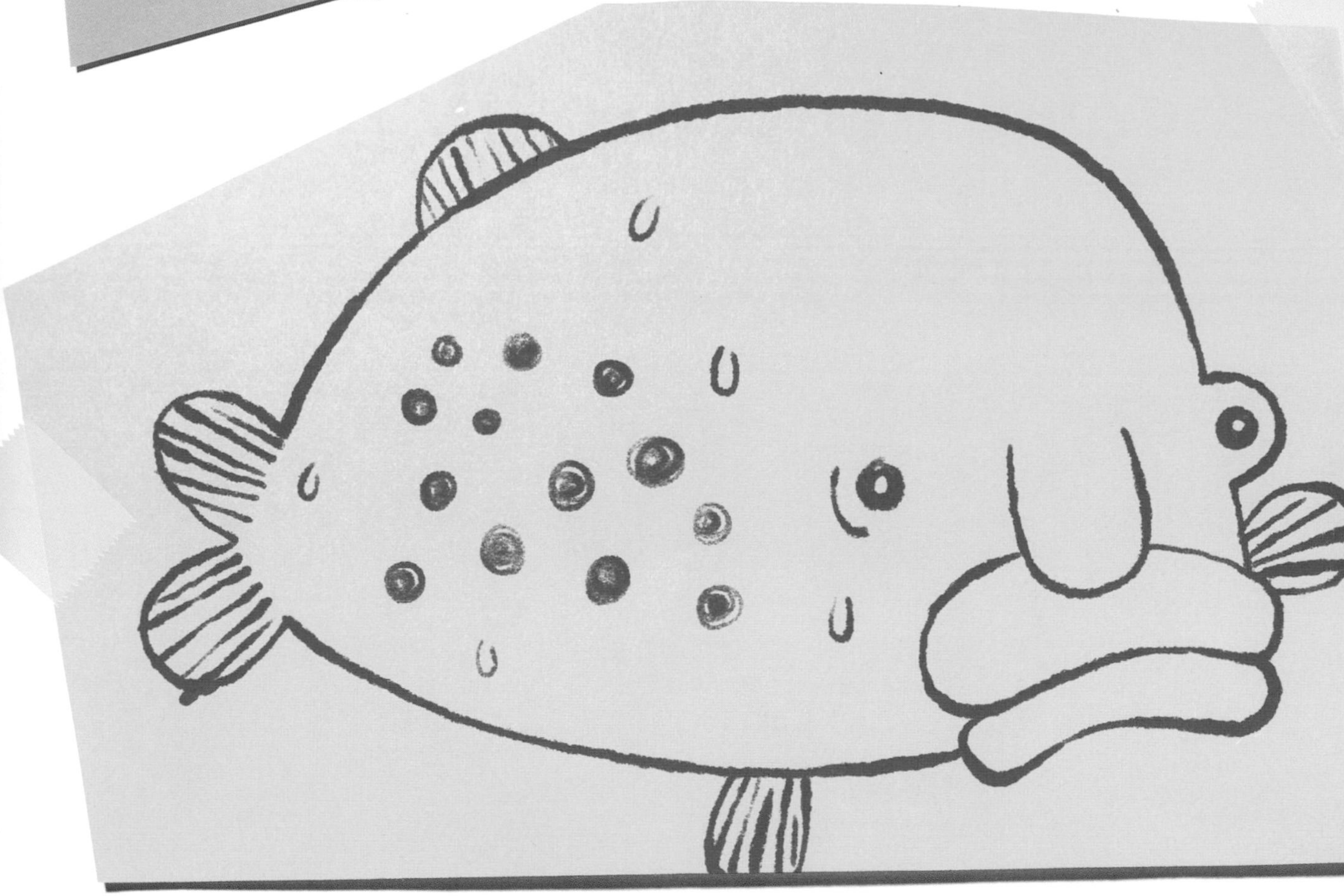

All right. All right.
I'm ready...

If the blobfish stood on its hind legs to eat berries . . .

it would be a gerenuk.

You have got to be kidding me.

Facts about Animals

Mammals

Mammals have hair and feed milk to their babies.

They can be very chatty.

Birds

Birds have feathers but do not have teeth.

They never color inside the lines.

Amphibians

Amphibians begin life in water and later also live on land.

They LOVE to dress up like princesses and pirates.

Insects

Insects have three-part bodies and outnumber all other animals.

They have VERY stinky feet.

Reptiles

Reptiles are cold-blooded and always have scales.

They never clean up their toys.

Fish

Fish breathe using gills and live in water.

They like to ride bikes after school.